Noddy on the Move

HarperCollins *Children's Books*

It was a sunny day in Toy Town and Noddy and Master Tubby Bear were in Noddy's little House-for-One.

"I wish we could go somewhere exciting," said Master Tubby Bear.

"Me, too!" said Noddy.

"But we never go anywhere," said Master Tubby
Bear, sadly.

Noddy looked out of the window.

"But we can!" he grinned. "I can move house!"

Master Tubby Bear was very upset.

"But Noddy! You can't leave Toyland," he cried.

"I won't leave Toyland," explained Noddy, laughing. "I'll go and live in another part of Toyland. I could live near the Ice-Cream Parlour –"

Tubby Bear smiled, "– and then you'd get ice-cream every day!"

Noddy was so excited, he couldn't wait to find a new place to live.

"Will you help me, Tubby Bear?" he cried.

"Oh, yes!" said Tubby Bear.

"It's moving day for Noddy!"

Big-Ears was cycling peacefully down the road
when he heard the sound of Noddy's car.
　　Big-Ears couldn't believe his eyes.
Noddy was pulling his little House-for-One
along on wheels.
　　"I'm moving!" said Noddy, proudly.

"But, Noddy!" cried Big-Ears. "What's wrong with where you used to live?"

"Boring!" laughed Noddy. "Now I'm going to find the PERFECT place."

And he roared off down the road.

"Hm," said Big-Ears, thoughtfully. "The perfect place, eh? I wonder!"

Noddy was so excited at the idea of moving
that he couldn't help singing:

> *Watch how I move*
> *My House-for-One.*
> *Life will improve,*
> *Moving is fun!*

Noddy and Tubby Bear went to tell Tessie Bear all about their moving plans.

"Why don't you live next door to me, Noddy?" said Tessie. "Then we can have tea together every day. We can feed my chickens — that's funny. Where ARE my chickens? They were here a moment ago."

Noddy and Tessie Bear hunted everywhere. But the chickens had completely vanished.

Then Master Tubby Bear opened the door of Noddy's little house.

"Here they are," he cried. "And they're making a terrible mess!"

"What can I do!" cried Noddy.

"You've put your house where they live," said Tessie Bear. "So they think it's THEIR house."

"But I don't want to live in a chicken house!" said poor Noddy.

"It's no good, Tessie," said Noddy, sadly. "I shall have to move."

Master Tubby Bear and Noddy climbed into Noddy's little car and set off again. But Noddy soon cheered up and he began to sing:

I'll find a spot
Meant to be mine.
I'll smile a lot,
Moving is fine.

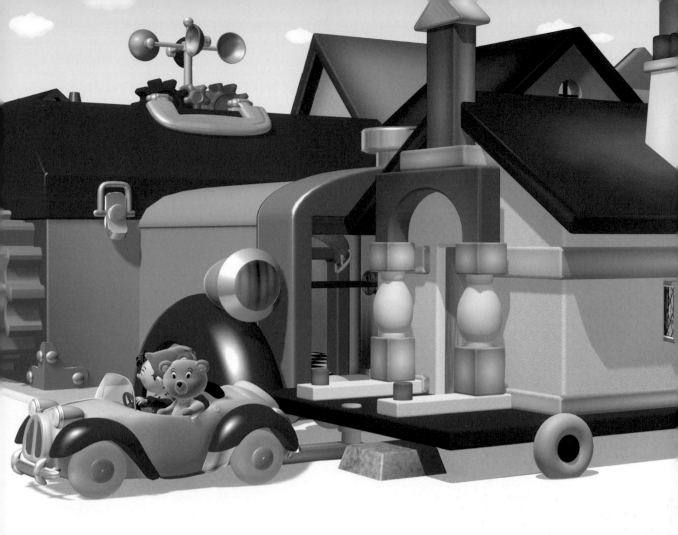

"There's Mr Sparks' garage," said Tubby Bear. "Why don't you live next door to Mr Sparks?"

"What a good idea!" said Noddy. "I'd love to have him as a neighbour. He's so good at fixing things!"

Noddy and Tubby Bear had just parked Noddy's house, when all of sudden, there was a terrific noise.
Boom-boom-WHHEEEE-OOOO!! Noddy's house bounced up and down.
"What is T-H-A-T?" cried Noddy.

"It's Mr Sparks, working in his garage," said Master Tubby Bear.

Noddy looked a bit worried.

"I expect I'll get used to it," he said. But he couldn't help thinking how nice and quiet it was where he lived before.

Then they heard the sound of a horn.

PAARP!

"What's happening?" said Master Tubby Bear. Noddy ran to the door and looked out.

There was Mr Sparks in his big tow truck.

"Oh, Mr Sparks!" cried Noddy. "I'm your new neighbour!"

"But Noddy!" cried Mr Sparks. "Your house is in the way! I can't get out of my garage!"

"I'm sorry, Mr Sparks," cried Noddy.

"We'll just have to move," said Master Tubby Bear. "Right away!"

"Never mind... We'll soon find the perfect place," said Noddy. "What about Town Square?"

"Why didn't we think of that before?" said Tubby Bear. "You'll see your friends every day. Everyone goes to Town Square."

Noddy was very happy. "It's going to be perfect!" he cried.

Noddy and Tubby Bear were looking out of the window at Town Square.

All of a sudden, there was a knock at Noddy's front door.

"My first visitor!" he said. "I wonder who it is?"

It was Mr Jumbo. He walked straight in.

And before Noddy and Master Tubby Bear could say a word, he took out a picnic hamper and began to unpack it.

"Mr Jumbo!" said Noddy, amazed.

"What are you doing?"

"I have a picnic on this spot in Town Square, every day," he said. "And now your house is here, I shall have to sit on your floor!"

"Oh," said Noddy, "I suppose so."

Perhaps Town Square wasn't going to be such a good idea, after all!

Just then, they heard loud, squeaky giggles getting closer and closer.

"Who's that?" said Tubby Bear.

CRASH!

A crowd of blue, green and pink Bouncy Balls whizzed into Noddy's little house and started bouncing all over it.

"Didn't you know?" said Mr Jumbo. "The Bouncy Balls practise bouncing here in Town Square, every day."

"But I live here, now," said poor Noddy.

"That's not going to stop the Bouncy Balls," said Mr Jumbo.

"NODDY!" shouted a voice.

Oh, dear! More trouble. It was Mr Plod.

Noddy opened his door.

"Move in the name of Plod!" said
the policeman, sternly. "Town Square
is a no-house-parking-zone!"

Noddy looked at Mr Jumbo, spilling crumbs on his clean floor. He looked at the Bouncy Balls, whizzing in and out of his windows. And he looked at Mr Plod's cross face.

"All right," he said. "I really wanted somewhere a bit less CROWDED..."

But it wasn't that easy. Everywhere seemed
to be full up.

Some time later, Big-Ears met a very tired
Noddy and Tubby Bear driving down the road.

"Still moving house?" asked Big-Ears.

"We've been moving ALL DAY!" said Noddy. "But
there were too many chickens and too much noise."

"And too many Bouncy Balls," said Tubby Bear.

Big-Ears thought for a moment.

"I do know somewhere you could try," he suggested. "A very pretty place. With no chickens. And no Bouncy Balls, either."

Wearily, Noddy and Master Tubby Bear followed Big-Ears. And a few minutes later they arrived...

They were back exactly where Noddy had always lived!

"Oh, Big-Ears!" laughed Noddy. "It's the best place in the world."

"Are you sure?" said Master Tubby Bear.

"I've been moving all day," smiled Noddy. "And I know now that this place is PERFECT!"

First published in Great Britain by HarperCollins Publishers Ltd in 2003

10

This edition published by HarperCollins Children's Books
HarperCollins Children's Books is a division of HarperCollins Publishers Ltd.

Text and images copyright © 2003 Enid Blyton Ltd (a Chorion company).
The word "NODDY" is a registered trade mark of Enid Blyton Ltd. All rights reserved.
For further information on Noddy please contact www.NODDY.com

ISBN: 0 00 715678 2

A CIP catalogue for this title is available from the British Library.
Visit our website at: www.harpercollinschildrensbooks.co.uk

Printed and bound by Printing Express Ltd, Hong Kong

make way for NODDY ™

Collect them all!

Noddy and the Treasure Map
ISBN 0-00-721056-6

Noddy's Pet Chicken
ISBN 0-00-721057-4

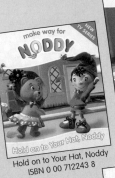

Hold on to Your Hat, Noddy
ISBN 0 00 712243 8

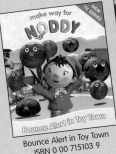

Bounce Alert in Toy Town
ISBN 0 00 715103 9

The Magic Powder
ISBN 0 00 715101 2

Noddy Builds a Rocket Ship
ISBN 0-00-721058-2

Goblins Above
ISBN 0-00-721059-0

Noddy and the New Taxi
ISBN 0 00 712239 X

Noddy's Perfect Gift
ISBN 0 00 712365 5

A Bike for Big-Ears
ISBN 0 00 715105 5

**And send off for your free Noddy poster (rrp £3.99).
Simply collect 4 tokens and complete the coupon below.**

TOKEN

Name: _____

Address: _____
_____
_____

e-mail: _____

❏ Tick here if you do not wish to receive further information about children's books.
Send coupon to: **Noddy Poster Offer, PO Box 142, Horsham, RH13 5FJ.**
Terms and conditions: proof of sending cannot be considered proof of receipt. Not redeemable for cash. 28 days delivery.
Offer open to UK residents only.

Make Way For Noddy videos now available at all good retailers.

UNIVERSAL